The Many Hats of
Mr. Minches

by Paulette Bourgeois

illustrated by
Kathryn Naylor

Stoddart Kids

*We acknowledge the Canada Council for the Arts and the Ontario Arts
Council for their support of our publishing program.*

First published in 1994 by
Stoddart Publishing Co. Limited

Published in Canada in 1997 by Stoddart Kids,
a division of Stoddart Publishing Co. Limited
34 Lesmill Road
Toronto, Canada M3B 2T6
Tel (416) 445-3333   Fax (416) 445-5967
E-mail Customer.Service@ccmailgw.genpub.com

Canadian Cataloguing in Publication Data

Bourgeois, Paulette
The many hats of Mr. Minches

Hardcover ISBN 0-7737-2839-2
Paperback ISBN 0-7737-5703-1

I. Naylor, Kathryn.   II. Title.

PS8553.078M3 1994   jC813'.54   C94-930241-4
PZ7.B68Ma 1994

Printed in Hong Kong

To my father

K.N.

All her life, Dotty Rupert had been a serious,
shy and sensible girl.
But her secret wish was to be brave and wild and bold.
Only there never seemed to be a chance . . .
until the Minches came.

D otty was sitting on the wharf when a fog,
thick and salty as her mother's pea soup,
settled on the harbour.
When it lifted, a fleeting moment later,
a man and a woman with a steamer trunk and a
mangy mutt stood on the beach.

"Ahoy!" bellowed the man.

He wore a tattered oilskin and a sou'wester
with CAPTAIN printed across the brim.

"Ahab Minches," he said, "Call me Captain.
This is my wife, Ondine and our dog, Moby."

Dotty noticed something as fishy as a catch
left too long in the sun.
On the trunk, as plain as could be,
was printed "Fred and Martha Minches".
The mutt's tag read, "Jeff".

When the Minches told Dotty they were moving
into a fishing shack she pointed out— sensibly—
that the water would flood their house at high tide.

The Captain jumped up and down.
"Couldn't be better! We can fish for our breakfast
right from our beds."

The Minches owned nothing but hundreds
and hundreds and hundreds of hats. The hats
were as curious as the Minches themselves.

"Try on any hat you like," said Mrs. Minches.

"People around here only wear sensible hats,"
said Dotty, "when it's rainy or sunny."

But the Captain wouldn't hear of it.
He picked a sailor's cap and popped it
onto Dotty's head. "Now you're my First Mate!"

Until the moment the hat was on her head, Dotty Rupert
had said only serious things. But suddenly she was
talking gibberish. "Yo, ho, ho, and pieces of eight!
Avast, ye landlubbers!"

"That's it, girl!" shouted the Captain.
"You'll make a brave sailor, that's for sure."

All the way home Dotty swaggered as if, at any moment,
the earth might heave like an enormous wave.

"Blow the man down if this isn't silly," said Dotty
swaggering along Main Street. "It must be the hat."

The Captain found a dory and a dinghy
and hauled them to his shack. He stood at the bow,
singing and shouting into the wind. "Man overboard!
Aye, aye, Matey. Be that treasure, Jim Boy?"

Dotty helped swab the decks and polish the brass,
but they never went out to sea.

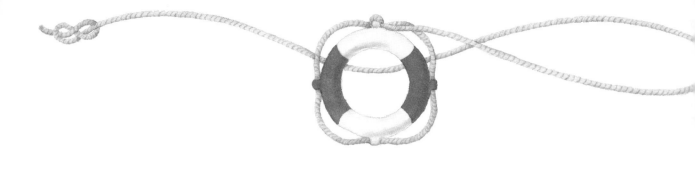

Dotty was drawn to the Minches
like a seagull to a fishing boat.
When the other children called them odder than
a pair of blue crabs, Dotty told them off.
When folks in town said the Captain was an old man
on a boat going nowhere, Dotty shrugged her shoulders.
And when the Welcome Committee snubbed Mrs. Minches,
Dotty baked her a cake.

One gusty day when even the seagulls came in
for shelter, Dotty warned, "Storm coming up, Captain.
Best batten down the hatches."

The Captain adjusted his hat.
"Nothing an old sea dog like me hasn't seen before."

But that night, when Dotty was tucked under her quilt,
she heard a scratching at her door.

It was Moby, the Captain's mutt.
He whined until Dotty followed him into the storm.

The wind hissed and whipped Dotty's nightgown
around her calves. The trees bent in the force
of the gale, and the waves battered the cliffs.

The fishing shack was swamped. Dotty scanned the wharf
and then looked out to sea. There!
The Captain and Mrs. Minches were clinging
to the dory, bobbing in the waves.

"I've got to get help," said Dotty.

But there wasn't time. The dory was sinking and she
could tell, the Minches couldn't hold on much longer.

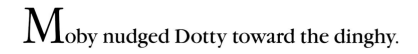

Moby nudged Dotty toward the dinghy.

"I can't do it, Moby. I'm not strong enough."
And then Dotty noticed the Captain's sou'wester
in the bottom of the boat. She pulled the hat
onto her head and started to row. She shouted
all the Captain's words into the wind. "Yo, ho, ho!
Aye Matey. Raise the mainsail. Lower the boom!"

Dotty's arms ached as she moved slowly forward.
The waves tossed her boat, but she sang
to make herself brave. Just as the Minches
were about to sink, Dotty threw them a line.

"Bring us in, Captain," shouted the Minches.

The next morning, the fog was as thick as custard.
Dotty found the Minches had packed their hats.
Mr. Minches was wearing a black sombrero
with turquoise stitching. Moby clenched a
red plastic rose between his teeth.

"Mr. Minches has had enough of the sea,"
said Mrs. Minches. "We're off to Mexico
where it's sunny and dry."

The Captain pushed a box towards Dotty.
His sou'wester was on top. "Choose the hat
that suits you best," he said as he waved goodbye.

TO DOTTY RUPERT
WHO IS BRAVE
AND WILD
AND BOLD

CAPTAIN

From then on, Dotty always wore one of
Mr. Minches' hats. She was particularly fond of
a ten-gallon hat that she wore fishing.
She'd lassoed a couple of feisty codfish and corralled
a school of halibut.

But whenever fog crept into the harbour,
she put on the old sou'wester and waited by the wharf
in case anyone needed a Captain
as brave and bold as Dotty Rupert.